Don't Call Us

by

Pat Thomson

Illustrated by Demitri Nezis

First published in 2008 in Great Britain by
Barrington Stoke Ltd
18 Walker St, Edinburgh, EH3 7LP

www.barringtonstoke.co.uk

ISBN: 978-1-84299-554-9

Printed in Great Britain by Bell & Bain Ltd

A Note from the Author

I am a fan of old black and white films. My best are the ones where a crime is set up and then it all goes wrong and the crime film turns into a comedy. Let's have a story, I thought, where someone is dragged to the edge of a crime. Can anything save him? Can something daft like a washing machine?! You'll need to read on to find out ...

Contents

Chapter 1
Hacker's Gang

"I was looking for you," Hacker said.

I'd been keeping out of his way and, for a week, it had worked. Now, he had found me. Hacker was big and nasty too.

"Hi, Shorty," he went on.

"Yes, Hacker?" I said, with a nice smile.

"Got a job for you. Bus shelter. East Street. Tonight. Nine o'clock. Be there." He talks like that. He thinks it makes him sound hard.

I hated Hacker. My name's not Shorty, anyway. It's Jack. We all hated him but he was king of the street. If he didn't like you, you knew it. I hated all Hacker's gang. Yesterday, his mobile rang in class.

"Sorry, sir," he said. "Important call." His gang cheered and yelled.

Mr Ford just held out his hand. Hacker gave him the mobile.

"Look after it," he said. "Cost a bomb. I bet it cost more than yours, sir." His gang yelled again.

They were the last people I wanted to meet anywhere. But at nine o'clock, I was there, at the bus shelter.

Chapter 2

In the Shed

Hacker was waiting for me at the bus shelter. He took me to the end of the street and we went over a wall and into a garden shed. It looked as if no one had used it for years.

"Come in. Sit down. Shut up," ordered
Hacker.

There were four chairs standing round a
packing case of some sort, and five people
there. There was Hacker and his best mate,
Gaz. Gaz was big, ugly and stupid. All he
could do was agree with Hacker. "Yeah,
right," he'd say. I think Hacker liked him
because Gaz made him look good.

Then there was Ratner. He also had a
chair. He was new. He was not only nasty
but dangerous. People said that he carried a

knife. Of course, that was fine with Hacker.
He liked to have him around. It fitted
Hacker's image of himself as a hard man.

There were two others, standing in the
darkness at the back of the shed. They were
Duffy and Belton, but I didn't really know
them.

I had the other chair.

"It's on for Friday night," said Ratner.
Donkey Jacket's got a darts match, so he'll be
out."

"Yeah, right," said Gaz, but he was puzzled.

We all knew who Donkey Jacket was. He handled stolen goods. He never stole them himself but passed them on. He wore a coat with big pockets. We would see him sometimes on a street corner. His hand would go into his pocket. A packet would change hands. He was someone to stay away from.

"Good," Hacker was saying. "Friday then. Down at his place. He's using the lock up."

"Yeah, right," said Gaz again.

The lock ups are garages with metal doors. They're all over our estate, away from the houses. Some are used, some have been empty for years.

"What's he got?" asked a voice from the darkness.

"A garage full of play stations! The new ones. Everyone wants one." Hacker was grinning. "Light to carry. Easy to hide. Simple to sell."

"Yeah, right," said Gaz.

"Just take small bags," Ratner told them. "Nothing anyone would notice. We can even fill our pockets."

"Stuff your pockets. Then fill a small bag. That's all you'll need," said Hacker.

"Yeah, right," said Gaz, a big smile on his ugly face.

"Because we don't want anyone thinking about what we're carrying," said Ratner. He'd done this sort of thing before.

Then I spoke. I wished I hadn't. "But his garage will be locked," I said.

"Clever boy," said Hacker. "Your job? Open the garage."

Chapter 3

I Don't Want To Do It

My heart sank. I might have known this was coming. My dad's a locksmith and locksmiths are honest people. They have to be.

"A locksmith you can't trust is no good to anyone," my dad would say. "People have to know you're honest." I couldn't use what I'd learned from Dad. He trusted me.

"What do you say, Shorty?" Ratner shifted his chair and came closer to me. "Are you with us?"

"I can't do anything. I really can't."

"Are you with us? Or are you against us?" Ratner stood up.

I heard the other two move forward in the darkness of the shed.

15

There wasn't a sound.

"I'll help if I can," I said, weakly.

"Yeah, right," said Gaz.

I didn't sleep much that night. I thought about Hacker's plan over and over again. We would go down to the garages in the late evening. There would be no one around then. There was a road behind the garages but there was no reason for cars to stop. People walked along there during the day, from the bus stop, but there were no buses at night.

17

The other side of the garages there were just fences and gardens. It would be OK if we made no noise at all.

Gaz would be look-out. That didn't make me feel any better.

Hacker said it was simple. I would open the lock of Donkey Jacket's garage. They would fill their pockets and bags. After that, we would each go a different way back to Hacker's shed.

I wasn't going to take anything. They couldn't make me do that. I felt sick just thinking about it. The awful thing was that if no one came along the road, it would probably work.

I fell asleep at last but my dreams were horrible.

Chapter 4

The Garages

The next two days were weird. Hacker stayed away from me. Gaz blanked me, too, but he was too stupid to remember who I was. Ratner came up to me at break.

"We don't want to be seen together," he said, "but I'll wait for you after school. I'll

walk you past the garages. Take a look at
the lock." Then he was gone.

When I came through the gates that
afternoon, I saw him. He was leaning on the
wall, waiting. When he saw me, he set off. I
went after him, keeping well behind. The
sick feeling came back.

We walked through the estate. Ratner
turned down an alley that came out behind
the houses. There were the rows of garages.
They were in blocks of six and I could see the
road between the blocks. Cars were speeding

past. The drivers could only see the backs of the garages. I looked at the garages again.

They had been there since the estate had been built. They were some way off from the houses. Some of the doors were open, some broken. I could see a lot of junk in one or two. I knew people put their old stuff in these garages and parked their cars in the street outside their houses, because they didn't want to walk that far. Some were locked, with normal padlocks. Easy locks. Why did Hacker need me?

Ratner was looking at me. "It's the one with the blue paint," he said. "Let's take a look."

We walked past slowly. I saw the peeling paint. I saw the padlock. It had some frayed rope hanging from it. I was puzzled. Hacker could have opened that himself. Then I saw the real lock.

It wasn't easy to see. Your eyes went to the bright new padlock. Just below, however, was a small lock. The newest sort. Top of the range. It was just about hidden by the

frayed rope. Someone didn't want anyone to see that lock.

Ratner walked on and I followed. At the end of the block, he turned and went down to the road. We stood in the empty bus shelter.

"Can do?" he asked.

"Sort of," I said. "But listen, locks like that are linked to the Police."

"As if!" Ratner smiled, showing all his small, sharp teeth.

He was right. Donkey Jacket might use a good lock but no way would he have it linked to the Police Station.

"It's too hard." I just had to get out of this. I sat down.

"There's a master key for that sort of lock, isn't there?" said Ratner. "Any good locksmith would have one."

Trust Ratner to know that.

"Yes," I said, "but Dad locks all that sort of stuff in the safe."

27

"So?" said Ratner. "You can open the safe."

He was standing over me, very close, his hands in his pockets.

"Yeah," I gulped.

"Good." Ratner gave a nasty grin. "We don't want you to get hurt, do we?"

A bus came along and he got on. I was left alone in the bus shelter. Panic time. It began to rain.

Chapter 5

Hacker's Mobile

Sometimes, you feel as if there is a dark cloud in your head. That was me when I got home from school.

I couldn't eat my tea. "You OK, Jack love?" asked Mum.

Dad had a big job on. He wasn't getting back until late. After tea I went straight up to my room.

"Got a lot of homework," I lied.

"Good lad," said Mum and I felt even worse.

On Friday morning, Ratner didn't come to school. I hoped he had been run over by a bus. Hacker was there. He had this crazy new ring tone on his mobile. He had recorded a police siren and someone shouting, "Help! Help!" It went off in class, of course.

Mrs Rush went white. The girls screamed and covered their ears. It was really loud.

Mrs Rush doesn't know Hacker very well yet. "I'm sure you didn't mean to do that," she said, "but I must keep your phone until after the lesson. There are times when we all must turn our phones off. It's a school rule."

"Yeah, right," said Gaz and the gang cheered.

31

"I'm sorry," said Hacker. "I get so many calls." He handed it over with a polite smile.

A moment later, the awful, loud ring tone went off again. I saw Duffy with his mobile under the desk. They had set her up.

"Oh, goodness," shouted Mrs Rush. "How do you turn it off?"

"I'll do it for you," said Hacker. "You won't be able to."

"Yeah, right," said Gaz.

Mrs Rush was now red in the face. In all the noise and the fuss, she didn't seem to see what had happened. Hacker had his mobile back.

Hacker and his gang stayed away from me all day. Hacker just nodded when we passed. When I got off the bus at the end of my street, however, Ratner was waiting.

"All OK for tonight?" asked Ratner. He didn't look at me.

"Yeah," I croaked.

"See you, then. If you don't turn up, I'll come and get you."

"Yeah, right," I said to his back.

Chapter 6

The Master Key

"I'm going round to Grandma's this evening," said Mum. "Will you be all right, Jack love?"

"Yes," I mumbled. "I may go to my mate's later."

"Oh, good," smiled Mum. "Dad will be very late tonight. They have to get that job finished. It will be nice for you not to be by yourself."

So that was that. There was no one else in the house. Just me and the safe. I went into Dad's workroom. The safe was behind the door. I didn't want to open it but I knew the numbers. The date of my birthday. I hated doing this to Dad.

Click, click. Stop. Click, click. Done.

What was that? I stood very still. No, it was nothing. I opened the safe door and took out the master key. I was angry with myself but I also felt afraid. I shut the safe again. I had to go.

Everyone was there in the shed. Hacker looked on edge. He walked up and down. Duffy and Belton were talking softly together. They seemed nervous, too. Gaz stared into space. Ratner was leaning against a bench, looking at each of us. He didn't move but his eyes flickered over us. I was shaking. I mean, really shaking.

They'd all got dark coats with big pockets. I think Gaz was wearing his dad's coat. Gaz is wide but his dad is as wide as the High Street. It looked as if he was wearing a tent. Hacker, Gaz and Ratner had caps with the peaks pulled down. Duffy and Belton had hoods. I had my light zipper. My face was white.

"Got what you need?" Ratner was talking to me.

I nodded. I couldn't speak.

"Yeah," said Hacker. He shot Ratner a sharp look and took charge again. "Listen up! The garages. Go one by one. Got that? When we get there, Gaz stands between the blocks of garages. He watches the road. There will be lots of cars."

"Yeah, right," said Gaz. "Cars on the road."

"Shut up!" said Hacker. "The cars won't stop. No problem for us. If," he said, grabbing Gaz by the front of his big coat, "if anyone WALKS along the road, tell us."

"Yeah, right," said Gaz. "Anyone who walks."

"But don't panic. They won't pass the garage doors. If we don't make any noise, we're safe. Then, Shorty opens the garage. We load the bags."

"Yeah, right," said Gaz. "And pockets." He patted his pockets. It made quite a breeze. A tent in a gale.

What was I doing here? It was crazy.

"Let's go," said Hacker.

43

Chapter 7

The Job

Suddenly, we were off. This was the real thing. I stood in the doorway of the shed and looked out. There wasn't a sound and the air was cold. Duffy and Belton brushed past me and melted away into the darkness. Hacker and Gaz went off together. I felt Ratner behind me, so I set off, walking fast. I went the long way round, twisting and turning, going back on my own tracks. Ratner was always behind me. I got to the blocks of garages.

Hacker came out of the shadows

"OK, Shorty?"

I nodded.

"Gaz, get ready."

Gaz moved to the gap between the blocks. He was looking back at us, not at the road. He was useless.

Ratner gave me a push. Duffy and Belton stood behind me. Hacker was on one side of me and Ratner was on the other. I took the master key out of my jacket.

It was easy. Just too easy. We heard the click as the master key worked. I zipped it back into my jacket. "Can I go now?"

Ratner shook his head.

"You stay here," he said. "Open the door, Hacker."

Gaz came and stood with the rest of us as the door swung up. Someone had oiled it not long ago and it rose smoothly without a sound.

We all gazed in. Washing machines. Rows and rows of washing machines, neatly stacked up. The garage was full of them. Only Gaz spoke.

"They're big," he said, patting his pockets in a puzzled way.

"Yeah, right," I said softly. "Someone gave you the wrong tip-off, Hacker."

Ratner started to speak and then stopped. "Car," he said. "Car stopping."

Duffy looked round the corner of the block. "Police car," he breathed.

Chapter 8

Yeah, Right

"Stay still!" snapped Ratner.

We did. We heard the brake go on. We heard the engine stop. We heard the windows slide down. We heard the sound of low voices. We even smelled the smoke from

their fags. They had stopped for a quick puff.
We just stood there, still as posts.

Then we all jumped. There was a loud,
shocking noise. A police siren and someone
shouting "Help! Help!" It was Hacker's crazy
mobile again!

I heard the car doors crash open. At the
same time, Ratner yelled, "Run!"

I don't know how I got home. I remember
throwing myself over a fence. I remember

going through a hedge. I remember jumping our gate.

The house was still dark. Lucky, lucky, lucky! I put the master key back in the safe. By the time Mum and Dad got back, I was in bed.

They were puzzled that weekend. I offered to go shopping with Mum. I helped Dad to clean the windows.

"All right, Jack love?" asked Mum.

"Yeah, fine," I replied.

In fact, I didn't want Monday to come. I had made up my mind. If anything like that happened again, I would tell Dad. It wasn't worth it. I'd had my warning.

As it turned out, Monday was OK. I was in the yard having a kick-about when Hacker came and stood very near me.

"You don't know me," he hissed. "Just blank me, and the others. The police have got Donkey Jacket. He's in big trouble." He looked round to see no one was near, then added, "We were never there."

I nodded. That was fine by me.

I expect Hacker's changed his ring tone. I don't really know because I never saw his mobile in class again, but I think so.

Yeah, right. I expect he did.

Barrington Stoke would like to thank all its readers for commenting on the manuscript before publication and in particular:

Joseph Ball

Roisin Banks

Jade Cheneau

David Clark

Emma Collingwood

Amanda Critchfield

Amy Ertan

David Hill

Aoife Kelly

Helen Oates

Eva Phillips

Kristal Phillips

Jordan Piper

Bernadette Redford

Brittany Salt

Claire Shardlow

Moira Slater

Jake Swapp-Sweet

Alex Tuffy

Becky Walker

Become a Consultant!

Would you like to give us feedback on our titles before they are published? Contact us at the email address below – we'd love to hear from you!

info@barringtonstoke.co.uk
www.barringtonstoke.co.uk

Great reads – no problem!

Barrington Stoke books are:

Great stories – from thrillers to comedy to horror, and all by the best writers around!

No hassle – fast reads with no boring bits, and a story that doesn't let go of you till the last page.

Short – the perfect size for a fast, fun read.

We use our own font and paper to make it easier to read our books. And we ask teenagers like you, who want a no-hassle read, to check every book before it's published.

That way, we know for sure that every Barrington Stoke book is a great read for everyone.

Check out www.barringtonstoke.co.uk for more info about Barrington Stoke and our books!